MoNTy'S
MAGNIFICENT
MANE

017

He is **not** amused.

So he shuffles

and shakes off the feathers...

… and stomps off to the waterhole to check his reflection.

"Monty!" says one little meerkat as he leaves.
"Remember to be careful of the…"

But Monty is too busy stomping to hear.

At the waterhole, Monty sees a little creature, with cheeky, twinkly eyes.

"My, what a wonderful mane you have," says the creature to Monty.
"In fact, some might say it's magnificent.
Why don't you come a little closer so I can see it better?"

Monty is very proud.
Fluffing out his mane, he
prances closer to his new friend.

He gets closer…

and closer…

and closer…

until…

It's a huge crocodile!

Monty leaps away, but not before losing
a big bite out of his beautiful mane.
"Come back here!" shouts the crocodile.
"I'm having you for my dinner."

So Monty runs as fast as he can for home.

When he gets there, Monty realises he's made a **terrible** mistake.
The crocodile has followed him all the way.

"Meerkats!" gloats the hungry creature.
"My favourite!"

Now, the meerkats might mess up his mane sometimes, but they're Monty's friends. He can't let the crocodile eat them!

But what can he do?

Then Monty remembers something he can do. Something that's really rather magnificent.

So he throws back his head…

and ROARS!!!

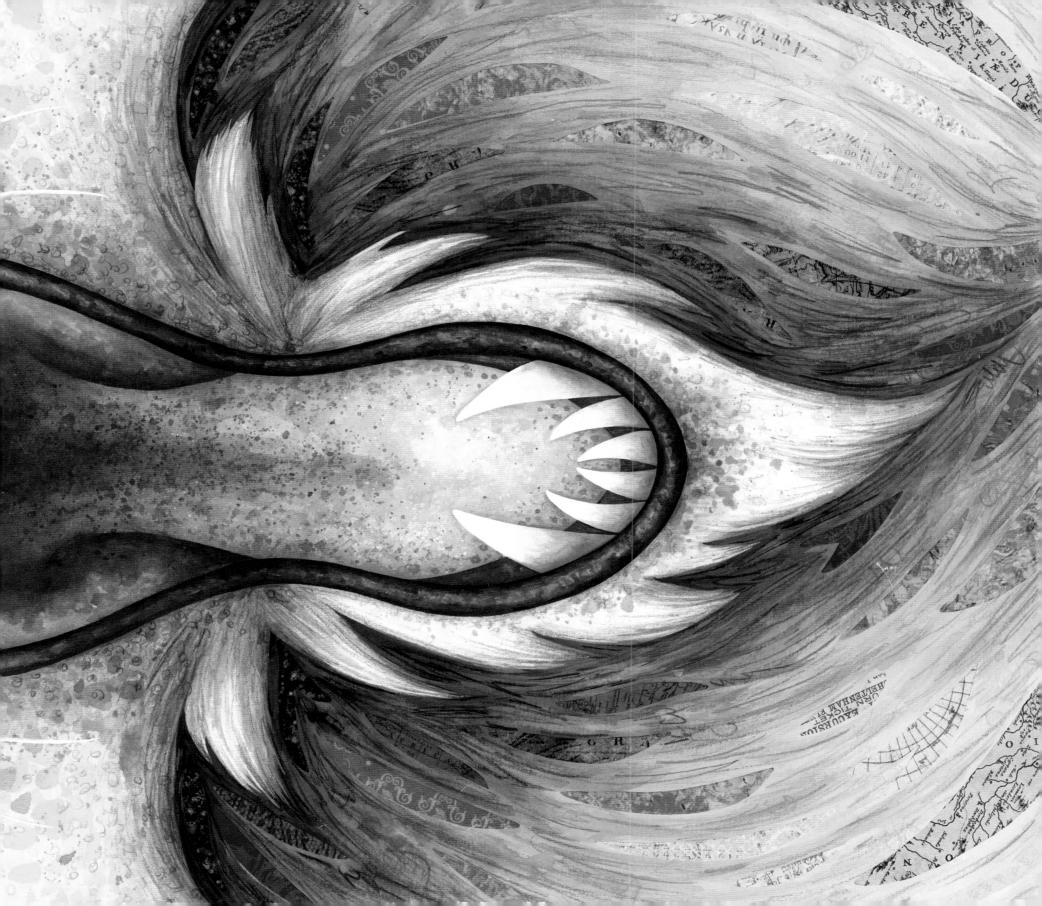

Monty's mighty roar sends the terrified crocodile
scuttling straight back to the river.

"You saved us!" cheer the meerkats.
"But look at your beautiful
mane. It's ruined!
That nasty crocodile took
a big bite out of it."

"Don't worry," says Monty. "My mane is fine as it is…"

"A duck so small can do nothing at all!"
they jeered.
   "I may be small," thought Duffle sadly,
"but there must be *something* I can do."
   He wondered what it could be.

Duffle looked around and noticed
Kingfisher perching on a reed.
He was just about to say hello,
when . . .

. . . Kingfisher suddenly took off and dived,
straight as an arrow, into the water.

"Kingfisher is small," thought Duffle, "but see
how well he dives. Perhaps I could do that, too."

"Look what I can do!" Duffle
called out to the other ducks.
He flew high into the air . . .

. . . and came down again
like a dropped stone.

Duffle hit the water so hard that he nearly
bounced off it!

"Ha, ha, ha, what did we say?"cried the other
ducks. "A duck so small can do nothing at all!"

Poor Duffle felt very foolish.
He climbed out on to the
riverbank, wondering
what to do next.

Duffle saw Heron, standing
perfectly still on one leg in
the shallow water.

   "What good balance she has,"
thought Duffle. "Perhaps I could
do that, too."

"Look what I can do!"
Duffle called, as he
stood on one leg with
his wings spread out.

He wobbled this way
and that and . . .

. . . landed flat on his beak.

"Ha, ha, ha, what did we say?" laughed the other ducks. "A duck so small can do nothing at all!"

Duffle crept off into the shade of a tree so that
the other ducks wouldn't notice his blushes.
Tap, tap, tap, went a sound above his head.

Looking up, Duffle saw Woodpecker making
a hole in the trunk.

"What a strong beak he has," thought the
little duck. "Perhaps I could bore a hole, too."

"Look what I can do!" Duffle called out to the other ducks. He flew up into the tree and perched on a thick branch. *Peck, peck, peck,* he went at the wood. "Oops," he cried as he lost his balance. Duffle toppled from the branch and . . .

. . . fell to the ground.

"Ha, ha, ha, what did we say?" cackled the other ducks. "A duck so small can do nothing at all!"

All the ducks were paddling and splashing in the
river, but poor Duffle decided to hide in the rushes
until they left. That way he wouldn't have to listen
to their sniggering.

"I'm good at nothing," he thought. "I'm just a small, useless duck." And a tear rolled down his beak.

For a long time, Duffle could still hear those ducks quacking with laughter. It seemed as though they would never leave.

"I'll stay here just a bit longer till they get tired of it," he thought. But as he listened, he realised something.

The ducks weren't laughing at him.
They were quacking in alarm!

Duffle paddled over to see what all the fuss
was about. It seemed that a duckling had got
stuck in a tiny hole in the riverbank.

"Oh, please get him out," begged the duckling's mother.

"We will," said the other ducks, but it was no good.

They were just too big to squeeze into the hole.

All except for Duffle.

"Let *me* try," he said and, because
he was so small, he was able to reach
right in.

It didn't take him long to
rescue the trapped
duckling.

"Good old Duffle!" cried one duck.

"None of us could have done that," said another.

"A duck so small *can* be useful after all!"
quacked a third.

"Oh, it was nothing," blushed Duffle. And,
though he was only a little duck, he felt bigger and
stronger than them all.

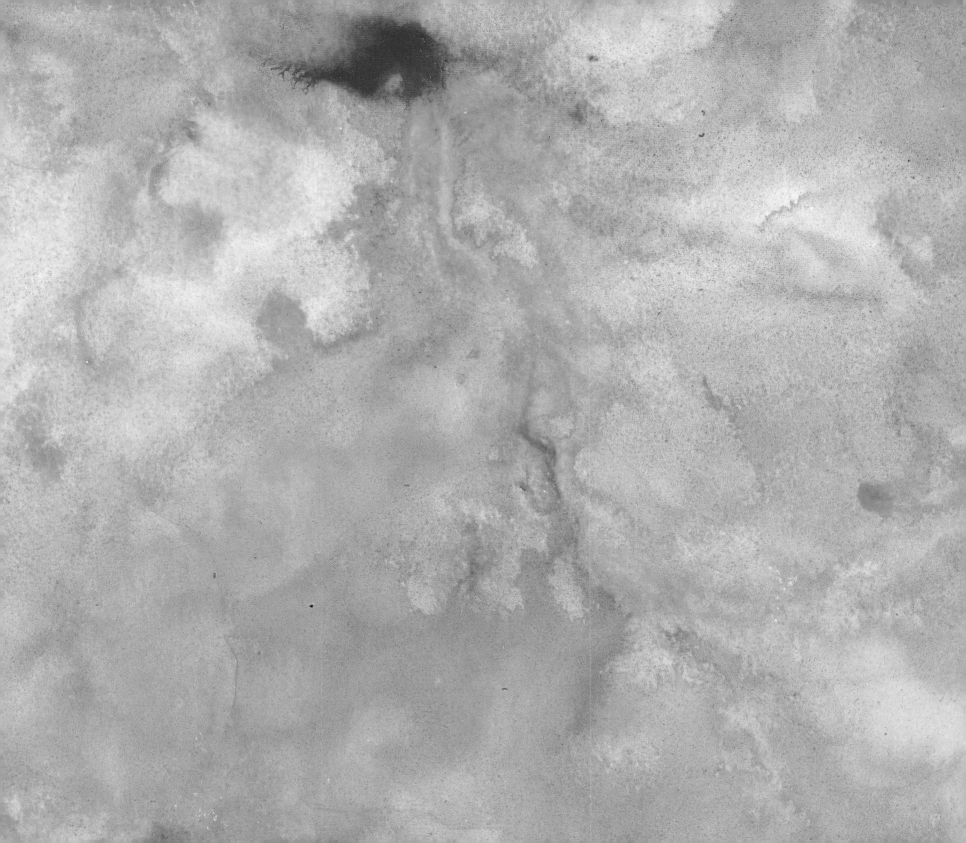